Damsen longs for the warm light beyond the castle walls. Brave Cnite Caerles seeks her hand, but her father the King has set a price: *You want Damsen. I want the Throme of Sherill. Find it for me and I will give you anything you want.* And so begins a quest that will wind from the Mirk-Well of Morg to the borebel pits to the Floral Wold to the Dolorous House of a dead Doleman and, finally, to the Western Wellsprings, where the answer to Everything lies . . .

A MagicQuest Book

The Throme of the Erril of Sherill

PATRICIA A. McKILLIP

with
**The Harrowing of the
Dragon of Hoarsbreath**

Illustrated by Judith Mitchell

TEMPO BOOKS, NEW YORK

THE THROME OF THE ERRIL OF SHERILL

A Tempo Book / published by arrangement with
Atheneum

PRINTING HISTORY
Atheneum edition / 1973
Tempo edition / January 1984

ISBN: 0-441-80839-5

Tempo Books are published by The Berkley Publishing Group,
200 Madison Avenue, New York, New York 10016.
Tempo Books are registered in the United States Patent Office.
PRINTED IN THE UNITED STATES OF AMERICA

To Kathy and Michele
and Lorene

The Throme
of the Erril of Sherill

ONE

The Erril of Sherill wrote a Throme. It was a deep Throme, and a dark, haunting, lovely Throme, a wild, special, sweet Throme made of the treasure of words in his deep heart. He wrote it long ago, in another world, a vaguely singing, boundariless land that did not exist within the kingdom of Magnus Thrall, King of Everywhere. The King had Cnites to come and go for him, and churttels to plant and harvest for him, but no Cnite had ever looked up into the winking morning sky and seen Sherill, and no churttel had ever looked at the rich clods of earth between his

boots and seen the Erril's world. Yet the Erril, long, long ago, wrote a Throme of singular and unsurpassed beauty, somewhere in his own land called Sherill, and the dark King of Everywhere desired that Throme.

The house of the King was a tall thing of great, thick stones and high towers and tiny slits of windows that gleamed at night when the King paced his hearth stones longing for the Throme. He had a daughter who sat with him and wept and embroidered pictures of the green world beyond the walls, and listened to her father think aloud to the pale sunlight or the wisps of candleflame.

"Who knows?" he would say. "Oh, who knows where lies the Throme, the Throme of peace, the Throme of loveliness, the dark Throme of Sherill? I must have it. If I had it, the most precious of all precious things, my heart would be at rest in its beauty, and I could stop wanting. If I had the Throme, I could wake at mornings knowing it belonged to me, and I could be content with the simple sunrise and the silly birds."

The King's Damsen would lift her hands and let them fall again into her lap. "There is no such thing. There is no Throme. Everyone knows that."

"Bah. Everyone is a fool."

And a tear would slide down the still face of the King's Damsen, and plop and twinkle on her hands. Her long hair was the color of pale sunlight, and her eyes were the color of long, motionless, uninterrupted nights. Somewhere beyond the dark stones was a moon-haired Cnite who loved the sad, sighing Damsen of the King.

That Cnite came one night to the house of Magnus Thrall. Damsen, who from the high window had seen the churttels come and go, and the daylight come and go, saw the Cnite ride across the fields of Everywhere and thump on the drawbridge of the house, which shut itself up at night like a grim, wordless sprite. Her sad, sighing heart gave two quick beats. Magnus Thrall, wearing a circle in the stones in front of a skinny, dancing elf of a flame, stopped.

"Who thumped across my drawbridge?"

"It is your Chief Cnite Caerles," said Damsen, and her voice was like the low, clear ripple of water across stones.

"Ha!" said Magnus Thrall. "I know what he has come for. But he cannot have you because I need you. If you go away, I will be here alone in these dark, dank walls. I need to look at your sad face. It comforts me."

A tear dropped onto Damsen's needlework and winked like a jewel among the bright threads. She looked towards the door at the sound of footsteps. They came through dark halls and empty rooms and lightless winding staircases towards her, for the King had shut up his house so that he could wail and wish alone. Spiders wove tapestry on the cold grey walls, and dust gathered, motionless, on the stone floors. The footsteps stopped at the doorway, and the Cnite Caerles stood in it, looking in at the warm fire, and the King, and Damsen with her eyes like cups of sweet, dark wine. He smiled at her eyes, and they smiled back, sadly, beneath their tears.

 8

"Go away," Magnus Thrall said.

"I just arrived," Caerles said reasonably. "My horse is in your disused stable. He is tired and I am tired, both of us having followed the sun and the moon to get here."

"You are welcome," said Damsen.

"You are not," said Magnus Thrall. "Besides, we have no room for you."

"I will rest content on the cold stones," Caerles said, "and in the morning I will come and ask something of you, and then I will leave you."

"I will give you an answer now," said the King. "No."

Caerles sighed. He stepped into the room. It was thick with fur beneath the foot, shining here and there with gold or silver, or dark, polished wood. Damsen's needlework hung on the walls. New flowers, pink and gold, and midnight blue, sat in water on the table. Such things would Damsen do in Caerles' house, bringing with her sad, lovely thoughts. He stood tall and straight before the King, his shirt of mail silvery as fish scale, his

sword and his shield of three moons at his side, proper and fair from his carefully brushed moon-colored hair to his gleaming, mouse-colored boots.

"I have come for Damsen," he said to her wet face turned towards him like a dawn-flower. "It is the time, in my loving, when I want no long, sunlit road between us, and no stone wall and closed door."

"You will leave without her."

"But why? You are growing a flower in the dark. You are shutting a rare stone up in a locked box."

"Why should I give my flower to you? You will shut her away in your own stones, to weep and sew beside your hearth."

"But I love her," Caerles protested. Magnus Thrall folded his arms and looked into the fire. Tears of pity welled in Damsen's eyes.

"You know nothing of wanting," said the King. "You know nothing of the gnawing beast of wanting, the ceaseless whine of wanting. You want Damsen. My wanting is greater than yours.

My wanting can make a great house empty, can make a silly world empty. I want the Throme of Sherill. Find it for me, and I will give you anything you want."

Caerles' mouth opened. It closed again, and then the words in his eyes came to it. "There is no such thing as the Throme of Sherill," he whispered. "Magnus Thrall, that is unfair. The Throme is a lie left from another king, another year. There never was a Throme. There was never a land called Sherill. There is nothing but the earth and the sky."

Magnus Thrall whirled away from the fire. "Unfair? What is unfair about wanting? Somewhere, somewhere, Caerles, you will find the Throme. Until then, I will grow my flower in the dark."

"You are cruel and loveless, you and your wanting."

"I know," Magnus Thrall whispered. "I know. The Throme is my hope. Find it for me, Caerles."

"But it does not exist."

"Find it for me."

"Find it, Caerles," said Damsen. He turned, his hands outstretched.

"But it does not exist!"

"I know. But find it, please, Caerles."

"Is there no reason in this dark, empty house? Magnus Thrall, you are King of Everywhere. You should open your doors, open your gates, open your hands and heart to me, to Damsen, to all your Cnites, to your vessels and churttels. Put tapestries on your bare walls, flame on your cold torches. Go into the green world and be content with what beauty is Everywhere, that you cannot see when your eyes are blind with wanting. Give me Damsen. I love her."

The dark King stood unflickering by the fire. "There is a price," he said, "on your loving. There is a price for the taking of Damsen from my hearth to yours."

"There should be no price!"

"Give me the Throme. Then you may have my Damsen."

The Cnite Caerles closed his eyes and sighed.

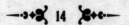

Then he went to the window where Damsen sat, the stars clustering about her hair. He took her hands and said sadly, "Will you wait for me?"

"I will," said Damsen, and a star fell down her cheek. "But oh please, hurry."

"I will. Though I do not know what use it is to hurry when I do not know where I am going, and when there will be nothing to find when I get there."

"I know," Damsen said sorrowfully. "My Caerles, you will be searching forever and I will grow old and ugly, and when you find it, you will not want me anymore."

"Yes, I will. I will be old and ugly too, then." He kissed her sadly, gently farewell. Then he said to Magnus Thrall, "I will find your Throme whether it exists or not. I will return with the price for her."

"I know you will," said Magnus Thrall. "That is why I set that price."

And so the Cnite Caerles came to leave the King's house by starlight, looking for the Throme of the Erril of Sherill. He stared up at the quiet

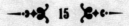

stars as he crossed the drawbridge, and they twinkled sympathetically on his upturned face.

"But it does not exist," he mourned to them. "Does it?"

TWO

And so the Cnite Caerles spent the night under a tree. He hated sleeping under trees. Trees whispered at night and dropped things on his face; trees wound underground and made hard knobs of their roots that gave lump in the back and crick in the neck. Trees let the sun too early in his eyes, and the sun would not go away. But worse than the sun was the Thing, that jumped out of nowhere onto the stomach of the Cnite Caerles.

"Oog," said Caerles and opened one eye. A child looked back at him, her hair in sweet, moist

tendrils down her back, her finger in her mouth. The other eye of the Cnite Caerles opened. "Child," he said cheerlessly, "why are you sitting on my stomach?"

"I have lost my dagon," said the child through her finger. Caerles looked at her motionlessly, unblinking in the sunlight.

"I, too, have lost something," he said finally. "I have lost my true heart's love, the well-spring of my deep heart's laughter, because I am sent on a hopeless quest from which I will never return. But that is no reason to go and sit on someone else's stomach."

"I want my dagon," said the child. She bounced up and down impatiently on the Cnite Caerles. Her eyes were blue as the tiny flowers that grew pointed like stars all around them. The Cnite reached out to still her, and she sat still, looking down at him, her eyes blue and fearless and certain as the true season's sky.

"Who are you?" said Caerles.

"I am Elfwyth. My dagon is Dracoberus."

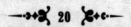

"Did you call him?"

"I called and called and called. And called. Who are you?"

"I am the Cnite Caerles, and I do not think I like small girls. Perhaps Damsen will have only sons."

Elfwyth took her finger out of her mouth. "I do not think I like you," she said sternly. "And if you do not help me find my dagon I will bounce up and down and I will cry."

The Cnite Caerles lifted her in his strong arms and stood up and set her on the ground, where she came barely higher than his knee. He folded his arms and looked down at her. She folded her arms and looked back up at him. Then, sudden as a falling star, came a tear rilling from the curve of her eye down to the corner of her mouth. Another followed, and her blue eyes were flowers with hearts of rain.

"Oh, please," she sniffed. "Oh, please find my dagon. Then I will help you look for what you have lost. Oh, please."

"Oh, please," Caerles said weakly. "Do not cry.

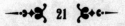

If you cry I will have to help you, for the love of the tears in my sweet Damsen's eyes."

"Oh, please find my dagon. I am lost and sorely sad without him, for I love him, and he loves me, and I will not go home without him."

Caerles gave a sigh sadder than the wind's sigh on moonless nights. "Oh, child," he said. "You are more annoying than a tripping tree root. What is a dagon?"

Elfwyth glanced up at him out of her still eyes. She sniffed. "It is a small animal. A little, little animal. And it has a little voice, and pretty eyes. You will not be afraid of it."

"I am afraid of nothing," Caerles said.

"And it will like you very much . . . if you find it while I am with you. It likes me most of all." She took the hand of the Cnite Caerles and turned him towards the morning sun. Flowers bent gently under her bare feet. "But it will like you, too, if you speak gently to it, I think. . . . It is my dagon, my Dracoberus, and it was a gift to me from seven—people. And then, if you find it, I will

love you, too." She smiled up at him, raising her fair face like a flower opening, and Caerles gave once more the wisp and whisper of a sigh.

"Thank you," he said glumly, and lifted her up into his great curved saddle.

They followed the sun until noon.

At noon the sun was a soundless, rearing lion frightening their shadows into littleness, a huge, golden dragon that was never still, the coin-gold heart of a blazing flower. At noon, they stopped to drink at the ice-colored sliver of a sheer stream. Elfwyth danced with her bare feet into the heart of the stream, among the polished stones and speckled sand, and as she splashed under the full eye of noon there came a roar like the waking of seven beasts in new spring. The Cnite Caerles ran to her, and the stream water sank deep into his mouse-colored boots. He lifted the child, holding her all wet against him, and then her voice shrilled into his eye.

"Oh, my Dracoberus!"

There was a flash like the wink of lightning. A

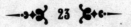

slender hound with violet eyes and fiery breath ran bellowing from the trees, and it was taller than Caerles' horse. Caerles stared motionless at its coming, while the child Elfwyth wriggled against him and his horse behind him reared and whimpered. Behind the hound rode seven men in seven colors, each with an eye ablaze on his breast, and a spear, ice-tipped, in his hand. Elfwyth twisted eagerly in the Cnite's arms.

"Oh, let me go—" she cried, and slithered like a fish into the water. She ran across the stream to the fiery hound and the sudden hiss of its breath over her head came at Caerles in a flood of flame. He sat down in the water. Seven men gathered at the water's edge. Seven spears formed a gleaming crescent above the Cnite's heart. Elfwyth hugged the neck of the whimpering hound. She kissed its violet eyes and turned her head.

"If you hurt the Cnite I will cry."

Caerles looked up at the still faces and fish nibbled at his fingers. He said between his teeth, "I do not like small girls."

"Go and kiss him thanks," Elfwyth said to the great, frolicking dagon.

"I do not want to be thanked," said the Cnite.

"You are afraid of my Dracoberus."

"Yes."

"You told me you were afraid of nothing!"

"Elfwyth, Elfwyth," said a man in scarlet, "it is not good for a small girl to mock a grown man. Who is this one?"

"I do not know. I found him beneath a tree and I bounced on him until he came with me to find my dagon."

The seven spears rose, flashing like birds. "We are the Seven Watchers of the child Elfwyth of the Erle Merle. We will bring you to him in thanks for his child, and you will be bedded in soft silk and washed in wine, if you but give us your name."

Caerles rose from the stream. "I am the Cnite Caerles, and I am questing for the Throme of the Erril of Sherill."

The Seven Watchers looked at one another. "It does not exist."

"I know, but I must find it. Will the Erle Merle help me? If not, I will bed myself in soft grass, having already washed."

The Seven Watchers turned their mounts. "The Erle Merle is wiser than an oak tree at twilight, wiser than the pale moon at moon rise. If he can help you, he will."

Caerles went with them, and Elfwyth rode the flaming dagon Dracoberus, and the barred gates of the Erle Merle opened without the touch of a hand to welcome them. The Erle Merle was a tall, thin wraith of bones and pale skin and hair like the spun gossamer of spider's web. His eyes flashed like jewels, now emerald, now amber, and they smiled as the child Elfwyth came to hug his knees.

"I have found my Dracoberus!" she shouted into his rich robe. "Now you must give that Cnite the Throme of the Sherill of Erril."

"Erril of Sherill," said the Erle Merle, and his eyes as he looked up flashed blue sapphire at Caerles. His hand strayed thoughtfully among the tousled curls of Elfwyth's head. "You are my wild

28

child, and it was your Dracoberus and your Watchers and this Cnite who found you. Now go to him and give him your hand like a true lady and bring him gently into my house."

And that she did, gently.

When they had eaten much of thin, hot slices of rare meats and golden-crusted breads and sweet wines and fruits, the Erle Merle sat back in his chair and looked first at Caerles and then at Elfwyth. Above his head was a huge, unwinking eye that the sun burnt gold, and all down the lengths of two sides of his hall lesser eyes watched, pools of violet, green, silver.

"I do not know where the Throme is," he said. "Or where it is not. I only know that it is not here." He tapped softly at the rim of his cup with the crescent moon of his curved nail, and his eyes went limpid grey. "I may have a suggestion, but it will lead to danger."

"There is a woman who weeps, waiting for me in Magnus Thrall's house," Caerles said. "I do not know that word danger."

"So." The Erle Merle's eyes winked like pure

stars. "Then I suggest you look for the Throme of the Erril of Sherill at the Mirk-Well of Morg."

The Cnite Caerles stared into his emerald green eyes. He said in a voice two tones smaller, "But the Mirk-Well of Morg does not exist. It is a line in a song, a passage of a tale told to children by fire light. How can I go to a place that is not there?"

The Erle Merle looked back at him out of midnight eyes. "What better place to find a thing that does not exist?" he inquired, and Caerles sighed deeply from his heart's marrow.

"Then I will go there," he said.

The child Elfwyth bounced suddenly in her chair. "I will go with you," she cried, "and my Dracoberus will keep you from danger."

"A quest is no journey for a frail child," said the Erle Merle, and his voice was a wind's murmur in the still hall. "My child, a true lady would give thanks to a Cnite who had braved fire and water to please her. Good thanks would be to give him what he may need most."

Elfwyth looked at the Erle Merle. Her eyes grew

round and heavy in the colored light from the watching windows, and her voice grew thin and quivered. "But he is afraid of my Dracoberus."

"I do not think he would be if you lent him your dagon to protect him from the glooms and harshnesses of the Mirk-Well."

"But he has a horse."

"I have a horse," said the Cnite Caerles quickly. "And I need no thanks."

The Erle Merle turned his face to Caerles and the glow of his eyes was of sweet, wine-drenched amethyst. "Thanks must be given," he answered softly, "and who will receive them if you do not?"

The child Elfwyth sat still as a drooping flower. Then she lifted her fair head and sat straight in her straight chair. "You will ride my Dracoberus," she said staunchly. "And he will protect you. And when you are done, you will ride him back to me. I will lend him to you in thanks, because you came with me in the morning light."

The Cnite Caerles achieved a smile. "I will ride him back to you safely," he said fairly, "and for the

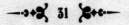

sake of my sweet Damsen, I thank you, for the protection of your Dracoberus against whatever dangers lie in the Mirk-Well of Morg, wherever they are, if they exist."

The child Elfwyth smiled back at him. She said anxiously, "Do not forget to bring him back to me."

"Oh, child," said Caerles from his deep heart. "There is no danger of that."

THREE

And that is how the Cnite Caerles left the hall of the Erle Merle by morning light, riding the violet-eyed, fire-voiced dagon Dracoberus instead of his true horse. He rode towards the path of the setting sun, where all darkness began, and the sun rode above him across the sky. At night, the eyes of Dracoberus glowed like violet stars, and his breath warmed the streaming air. He ate leaves from the trees and tender flowers newly opened, and he acquired a habit of licking the Cnite's face with his great, red, fiery tongue. He moved like a wind over plowed field and meadow,

and at the end of the second dusk Caerles knew they were lost.

"Though," he said reasonably as he dismounted, "I cannot be lost when I am going nowhere." And he was surprised when instead of earth beneath his foot, he felt a nothingness that continued in a dazing rush. He landed asprawl on the damp earth and found the violet stars looking at him from an unreasonable distance. "How," said the Cnite Caerles reasonably between his teeth, "can I possibly get where I want to go when I cannot go anywhere at all?"

The dagon whimpered down to him in sadness like a child, and Caerles could hear the thump of its great tail like a heart-beat on the earth above. Then of a sudden the burning violets vanished, and the Cnite heard a light Boy's voice in a lulling croon.

"Oh, I love you, I love you, I love you. . . ." And through his voice came the purry whine of the dagon and the thump-thump of its tail.

"Who is up there?" Caerles called. The voice

was silent. A dark face peered over the edge of the earth.

"Who is down there?"

"I am the Cnite Caerles. Will you help me?"

The voice was silent again. The night was silent but for the little voices of secret things that no eye could see. The trees lifted their great black heads against the stars and the wind curled through them, sighing.

"Is this your thing up there? This beautiful purple and red and grey thing?"

"It is the dagon Dracoberus that I was riding. Am I in the Mirk-Well of Morg?"

"No. You are in my borebel pit. Are you sure you are not a borebel?"

"I am not a borebel," said Caerles. "I am the Cnite Caerles of Magnus Thrall, questing for the Damsen of the King. I am cold and dirty and sore and hungry and I do not like your borebel pit."

"Well," said the voice. "Well. I think if you were not a borebel you would not be down there. It is a pit only for borebels. There is a long-toothed,

hoary-voiced, squinty-eyed borebel snuffling around my mother's house and I dug a pit to trap it. How do I know you are not a squinty-eyed borebel with a sweet voice to trick me?"

The Cnite Caerles closed his eyes. He opened them again and said patiently, "Do borebels ride dagons?"

"No. But I think you ate the Cnite who was riding this dagon, and now he belongs to no one. So I will take care of him, for he is more beautiful than anything I have ever seen and he loves me, too."

"I am not a borebel," said Caerles. "And that dagon was lent to me by the child of the Erle Merle to protect me from all danger with its swift speed and its flaming tongue, but I do not know what will protect me from a troublesome young Boy."

"Perhaps I will let you out," said the voice, "if you give me the dagon. Then I will have someone to sprawl on meadow-grass with, and explore deep caves, and dabble with in the river. If you

give me the dagon, I will know you are not a borebel, for a borebel never gives anything to anyone."

"But I cannot give you Dracoberus because he does not belong to me."

"Then," said the voice cheerfully, "you must be a borebel. Do not worry about your dagon. I will love him well."

The Cnite Caerles sat down on the damp earth of the borebel pit. "Boy," he said wearily, "I am a Cnite on a quest for the love of a wheat-haired, wine-eyed lady who is waiting with love for me. You will have the dagon to love but who will there be to love that lady if you do not let me out of this pit?"

There was the sound above of shifting leaves. "Well," said the voice, and again, "well." Then it said again cheerfully, "If you are truly a borebel, there is no lady and no love, so I will take your dagon. But do not worry. I will feed you."

The heads of the Boy and the dagon vanished, and the Cnite Caerles was left alone with the far-

away stars and the whispers of trees and the walls of earth rising around him. "Oh, my Damsen," he mourned softly to the memory of her, "will you still love a clumsy Cnite who falls into borebel pits?" And the Throme seemed as far from him as the star-worlds above.

Morning fell into the borebel pit onto Caerles' eyes, and he looked up and found a rope of sunlight up to the bright earth. He sat up and sighed for the ache in his bent bones and the thirst in his throat and the mud on his mouse-colored boots. Then he heard the whimper and frolick of the dagon and the high, sweet whistle of the Boy swooping like a bird's cry through the trees.

"Borebel," he called, "I have brought your breakfast. And then the dagon and I will run as far as the world's edge together, and shout louder than sound, and we will not come back until there is no more night. Borebel, Borebel, I have brought bread and porridge and milk, O Borebel. . . ."

And as he called and whistled, a strange noise tangled in his whistling: a snickering, snuffling,

snorting noise that came to the very edge of the borebel pit. And then of a sudden, it came down into the borebel pit, and the Cnite leaped out of its way. Across from him lay a tiny-eyed, long-toothed, bristle-hided borebel blinking its red eyes in astonishment.

"O Borebel," Caerles breathed, for the borebel, sitting, was as high as his chin. "Move gently, or I will kill you, and I did not set out to kill borebels."

The borebel snorted. Its eyes flamed suddenly blood-red with rage, and the Cnite drew his sword. The borebel stood up on its short-haired hind legs and the scream of its fury silenced the birds in the morning trees.

"O Borebel," said the Boy above them, and his voice quivered like a bow-string. "Look up."

The borebel looked up. The Boy dropped a great bowl of steaming porridge onto its squinty-eyed face.

The borebel danced and roared and splatted the porridge out of its red eyes and its long-toothed snout. The Boy dropped the end of a

rope down the pit-edge to the Cnite. The dagon Dracoberus howled at the other end. Red flame singed the borebel's hide. Then the dagon pulled with its might and Caerles slithered out of the borebel pit.

He stood free above the mournful borebel, all covered with earth and tiny twigs and the frayed ends of leaves. The Boy looked up at him, shivering in the sunlight. He was bone-thin and brown, with scarred knees and elbows and his eyes were round as twin platters on a white table.

"You are not a borebel," he whispered. The dagon licked the Cnite's face with a swoop of its tongue, then lay on his feet and thumped its tail.

"Boy," began Caerles. Then he stopped, and his anger faded away in the sigh of his breath. "No. I am not a borebel."

"I wish—I wish you had been. But I knew you were not. Are you going to be very angry?"

"You saved my life," said the Cnite, "in spite of the deep longing of your heart. I too have a deep longing for a special love. I cannot give you the dagon for a fearless-eyed child loves it, but I will

give you, for your sacrifice, whatever else you may ask of me."

The Boy licked his mouth. "Then may I have—" He stopped and swallowed. "Then may I please have your sword?"

The Cnite Caerles was silent. Little winds came plucking at him, springing away like teasing children. The great dagon rolled over and scratched its back on the bracken. He drew it finally from his belt and it flowed silver in the light and tiny jewels, red and white and green, winked in its hilt.

"It is yours," he said, "because you asked it of me. But why do you want it?"

"To kill borebels bravely with, when they come snuffling in my mother's garden. And then I will not have to dig any more pits."

Caerles gave him the sword. The Boy's eyes caressed it from pommel to tip and he smiled. "It is very beautiful. But not," he sighed, "as beautiful as the dagon beside me at night. And now, if you will come, my mother will give you some breakfast. And some water to wash with. . . ."

The Boy's mother shook the Boy for leaving the

Cnite overnight in the borebel pit, and then she hugged him to her, winking and blinking, for his quick wits, and then she shook him again for his request of the sword. Then she filled a heaping bowl of porridge for the Cnite and listened to the tale of his search. Then she said,

"There is no such thing as the Mirk-Well of Morg."

"I know," Caerles said. "But you see I must find it."

The Boy's mother shook her head. "Mirk-Well of Morg is a tale for old men and babies, not for great Cnites. Now, if I were you, which I am not, being simple and stout and motherly, I would look in the Floral Wold at the World's End. Now, there is a place for a Throme of beauty. A dreamer dreamed the Floral Wold, and it appeared, somewhere beyond the sunrise. I would go there. But then I am only a poor old woman with only half my teeth, and the Throme most likely does not exist. But I would go there, to the Floral Wold, if I were a brave Cnite with a loving, weeping woman. Eat your porridge."

The Cnite Caerles ate his porridge. Then he said, "I do not know where to go. The Erle Merle said nothing of a Floral Wold, but I cannot go to the Mirk-Well of Morg without a sword."

"It does not exist," said the Boy's mother, "and it was wrong of the Boy to ask for your sword."

"He would not give me the dagon," the Boy argued contentedly; "I would have taken that instead."

The Boy's mother ticked her tongue. Then she bent down and lugged a worn chest out of a spider-woven corner. She opened the lid and it wailed with age. A glow came from the chest like the milk-white eye of a lost star. "This my mother gave me," she said, "and her mother to her. It is the guiding light to the Floral Wold, the candle that illumines dreams." She lifted the star from the chest. It pulsed, softly white at the end of a staff, now petaled like a flower, now pointed like crystal, and the far heart of it was ice-blue. The Boy's eyes grew wide, twin stars from the star-wand winking in them.

"Oh, it is beautiful," he sighed longingly, and his

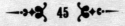

mother slapped his reaching hands.

"Greedy," she said, glowering. "Be content with the pure jewels in that sword." She gave the star to Caerles, and the longing came, too, into his voice.

"Oh, Lady," he said softly, "I am greedy, too, for that land where this grew. If it exists, then I think I will begin to believe that the Throme exists, too, somewhere beyond the sunrise, beyond the World's End."

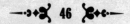

FOUR

And so the Cnite Caerles rode towards the World's End, with the glowing-eyed dagon bounding beneath him and the starlight of dreams ablaze at his side. And the rising sun traced a path of gold before him, and the end of the road lay in the secret heart of the Floral Wold. On the third day of his riding he came to a norange orchard.

The noranges grew full round, flaming orange and green among the warm leaves. Soft, sleepy winds drowsed through tiny specks of flowers, red, blue, yellow, white, dancing like stars across the orchard grass. The Cnite Caerles paused in

the noon shadow of a tree. He picked a norange and peeled it slowly. Green and gold flies with jewelled wings hummed around him at the scent of it. The sunlight dripped from leaf to leaf and pooled upon the green grass. Caerles ate his norange, piece by piece, and the sun weighed upon his eyelids, and the jewel-flies hummed a dream from hidden places. The green world slept beyond the orchard, lulled motionless. Watching it, the Cnite's eyes grew still, and the norange grew heavy in his hand.

He fell asleep beneath the orchard tree and dreamed a dream. . . .

A jingler came flickering across the meadowlands, one-half of him red, one-half white. The bells on his hood winked and tinkled in the lazy winds. He sang, his fingers plucking at a gold-stringed harp, his voice light and cheerful in a dolorous song:

> "I loved a lady once
> Beneath an orchard tree

*The fine lady Gringold
And she did not love me.*

*I sang my love to her
And she laughed at me
Fine-fingered Gringold
Beneath a norange tree.*

*Wake up and listen, Cnite
Wake and listen to me
Or you will taste of sorrow
Beneath that Gringold tree."*

He came to the edge of the tree's shadow, and stopped, looked down at the blinking Cnite and the yawning dagon. "Ho, Sire Cnite. Have you seen a lovely, light-fingered lady?"

"No," said Caerles.

"Then you are fortunate," said the jingler, and sitting down, he whirled a handful of harp-sounds light as butterflies into the air. His dark brows were arched in mockery, and smiles came and

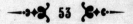

53

went in his eyes and tugged at the corners of his mouth. "She is a willful wicked woman, even though she is more beautiful than a redbird in flight, or a flower new-opened."

"I know a woman so beautiful," said Caerles. "She is the candle-flame in the dark room of my heart, and she loves me."

"Then you are very fortunate," said the jingler. "But no man in love with a true lady should sleep beneath this norange tree. Why are you not at her side?"

"I cannot be, until I find the deep Throme of the Erril of Sherill."

The jingler plucked three strings and sent a sad chord into the air. "Then you will never be with her, Cnite, for the Throme is a dream."

"That may be so, but I will find it."

"Where will you look for it?"

"In the Floral Wold, at the World's End."

The jingler laughed. "Then go back to sleep, Sir Cnite, and step into your dream for only then will you ever reach the World's End."

Caerles was silent a moment. The dagon licked idly at his hands, and watched the jingler out of quiet, violet eyes. "You may mock me," the Cnite said at last, "as I mocked the King who sent me on this hopeless quest. But I will not yield my true love to all the world's laughter. I will go where I must, find what I must to get that Throme, for that is the price of my loving. You also would do what you must, however impossible, to win your Gringold's loving."

"I do not love the Lady Gringold," said the jingler.

"Then why are you here beneath her tree?"

The jingler turned his face away.

There came a lady into the shadow. Her hair was wound in soft gold braids to the hem of her green robe, and her green eyes were smiling, full of hidden things. The wind shook her robe and from her came the sweet, light scent of noranges. She sat down beside the Cnite Caerles and touched his hands softly with her cool, fine fingers.

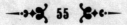

"There is one man left in this wide world with the dream of love. Do not let this jeering jingler wither the flame of your dream with his windy words. Tell me of your quest and I will help you if I can."

"I must find the Throme of the Erril of Sherill," said Caerles. He looked into the lady's eyes as he spoke, and suddenly there was no color in the world but the clear ice-green of them, and no sound in the world but the memory of her voice. Far away, beyond the world, he heard the jingler's voice in mockery:

> *"Wake up and listen, Cnite*
> *Wake and listen to me*
> *Or you will taste of sorrow*
> *Beneath that Gringold tree . . ."*

"I have heard," said Gringold, "of the King's Damsen. All she does is weep."

"Some ladies," said the jingler, "have a heart to weep from."

"A true love," said Gringold, "would not send a Cnite on such an impossible quest for which he will never return. Perhaps, fair Cnite, she does not want you to return."

"Some women," said the jingler, "know what it is to be faithful."

"She will have to wait a very long time. Perhaps even now the image of her moon-haired Cnite is fading, and there is some brown-haired, berry-eyed Cnite who caught her fading fancy as he passed beneath her window." The sweet voice of the Lady Gringold purred like the wind among the tiny flowers. "Perhaps she is no longer weeping. Perhaps she already has learned to laugh from a Cnite who is there beside her, not riding down a road with no end, searching for a Throme that is an old man's dream, a wicked King's wanting . . ."

Caerles drew a sigh from the wind's breath. He whispered, "There is a place in my heart you have hurt. . . ."

"Some women," said the jingler, "can touch a thing without hurting it."

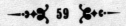

"All jinglers," said the Lady Gringold, "are tear-less and faithless and cruel." She took her eyes suddenly away from Caerles' face and the world came back to him, golden and drowsing in the afternoon sun. The jingler's smiling had gone from his eyes and his voice.

"I made a song of you, more beautiful than any song, and you laughed at it," he said. "I loved you and you mocked me, under your norange tree. And now you are holding this Cnite's hands, and talking to him in a voice sweeter than norange-juice." He turned away abruptly and folded his arms and stared across at the World's End.

"I waited for you," said Gringold, "one afternoon beneath this tree, and you did not come. And I like this Cnite and I will help him if I choose."

"I would not trust you," the jingler said to the sky, "if I were that Cnite. I did come, that afternoon, and you were not there."

"I was there!"

"You were not!"

The Lady Gringold folded her lips tightly. The jingler leaned back against the tree and began to pick at his harp, and watched the wind go by.

> *"Fair lady*
> *False lady*
> *There is no other kind*
>
> *Green norange*
> *Golden norange*
> *No other can you find."*

"Damsen is both fair and true," Caerles said slowly. "There is no berry-eyed Cnite. That is a dream woven of empty words."

"So is the Throme woven," said the jingler above his harp-strings. "And so is the Floral Wold."

"Then where shall I look?" Caerles mourned, and the dagon lifted its great head and whined in sympathy.

"Stop looking, and go back."

"No. The King's wanting will still be there. I will find it."

The Lady Gringold loosed his hands and sighed. "Cnite, you are steadfast. There was a song I heard long ago, when my tree was a slender, stirring thing, of a Throme haunting the dark, dank Dolorous House of a dead Doleman. Go there, and you may find it."

The jingler laughed. "What woman is worth the price of the step across that threshold?"

The Lady Gringold stood up slowly. She grew taller as she rose, so that her shadow touched the edge of the norange tree's shadow and flowed beyond it. "Jingler," she said gently, "it is not wise to mock too much the lady of a norange tree."

The jingler rose, too, and flung away his harp. His bells jingled wildly at his own sudden growing. "Nor is it wise," he said bitterly, "to keep a Noak-lord waiting beneath your tree."

"You are not a Noak-lord! You are only a silly jingler with a capful of bad rhymes."

"Can a jingler do this?" said the jingler, and he whirled a circle until he vanished and in his place a great, red bird bigger than the norange tree sucked the wind into its wings. The dagon rose and howled at it. The Lady Gringold laughed a spiteful note, and her hair streamed like threads of honey in the wind.

"I would rather have this moon-haired Cnite who can do nothing but dream. I will fly away with him to the World's End and leave a Noaklord beating at my closed gates—" And her streaming hair whirled about her, spinning into a green-gold bird with ice-green eyes that swooped, open-clawed, at the Cnite Caerles. The dagon hissed its breath of flame and the wide wings beat flame back at it. Caerles lifted his shield against the fall of the lady-bird and the golden talons closed about it, lifted him out of the shadow of the norange tree, lifted him above its branches, lifted him into the great blue of sky with the red bird blazing in pursuit.

And suddenly he dropped. . . .

He woke to twilight beneath the norange tree, and the quiet-eyed dagon licked his face. The sun had gone from between the grass-blades. The wind lay at rest beyond the blue hills. The noranges hung winking like jewels in the still trees. He looked at them and smiled.

"I had a foolish dream," he murmured, remembering. The dagon's tail thumped at his voice. The Cnite rose, yawning, the star-wand shining softly at his side, and reached for his shield. It was gone. And in the place where it had been there lay a gold-stringed harp.

FIVE

And so the Cnite Caerles rode to find the Dolorous House of the dead Doleman, the star-wand ice-white at his side, the gold harp gleaming at his back. And as he rode through the days, the winds hummed a deep, dark Throme without words of storm and purple cloud and sharp, cold rain. The storm came at last, like a black-cloaked king with a fanfare of thunder. Rain slid beneath Caerles' shirt of mail and ran across his face like tears. The dagon's eyes glittered in the flashing lightning. He howled at the wild winds, and they screamed back, sweeping away

across the wet world. Caerles stopped finally beneath a barren tree, blinking away the silver rain misting the coming night.

"Oh, dagon," he sighed, "any house will do for us tonight, a house of the living or of the dead. . . ." He moved away from the black-limbed tree and lightning split it from top to root. In the sudden, blazing light he saw a cottage white-walled against a hill, with a single window watching the night like an eye.

The dagon's paws sank deep into the wet road in its running, and its violet eyes were the only stars in the world. It whimpered as it reached the cottage door and the hearth-flame melted warm across the window. The door opened slowly; a single eye looked out at them through a crack.

"Who is there?"

"I am the Cnite Caerles," said Caerles through the rain in his mouth. "I am cold and wet, and I beg shelter from the storm."

The voice was silent a moment. "If you are a Cnite, where is your sword and your shield? And why are you riding that—that—"

"Dagon."

"Dagon. My mother said I should never speak to swordless Cnites riding dagons."

"I am looking for the Throme of the Erril of Sherill," said Caerles. "Child—"

"I am not a child," said the voice haughtily. "I am a young damsel. My name is Ferly. Your dagon has beautiful eyes. What is that star at your side?"

"Young damsel," said the Cnite, "I am searching for the Dolorous House of the dead Doleman, in which I may find the Throme. A child would let a Cnite drown in rain beneath the night sky while she chattered, but a true lady, such as the Damsen I love, would open her door and lead him graciously to her hearth fire."

The door opened farther, to Ferly's face. "Oh," she said slowly, and her long fingers clasped together. "Do you love the King's Damsen? Is she beautiful? Does she weep with love for you—is that why she cries? Are you questing for love of her? Why, you are all wet. Come in." She opened the door wide and smiled graciously. The wild

wind pounced like a cat across the threshold and set the hearth-flames fleeing. Caerles dismounted wearily and stepped into the house, leaving wet footprints on the stone floor. The damsel was lean and long-haired, her face flickering like an eager flame, her fingers and elbows jointed like smooth twigs. She pulled a bench in front of the fire for Caerles to sit on, and then she led the dagon into a shed beside the house. Then she sat down in front of the fire and looked at Caerles out of her quick, bright eyes.

"I know where the Dolorous House is," she said. Caerles, lulled by the warm, dancing fire, blinked awake.

"Where is it?"

"Ride down the road on your dagon, and the road will twist and turn three times, and on the third twist there is a hill, and on the hill is the black, crumbling, rotting House of the dead Doleman. It has great towers without doors, and walls like broken teeth, and when the moon is round, then strange, colored lights shine above the House, and strange shoutings come from

 72

beyond the walls. My mother says I must never go there, or one day I will vanish and no one will hear of me, ever again. They will only hear my voice crying from the dark towers when the moon is full." She shivered, and smiled up at the Cnite, her eyes cups of firelight. "It is very frightening. But I know a secret protection."

"What is that?"

She paused, thinking, her head tilted like a listening bird. "It is magic," she said softly. "And I would only give it to someone—someone on a pure quest for a wondrous love. You will have to tell me everything about your quest. And then perhaps I will help you."

So Caerles told her of the King's deep wanting, and of Damsen's weeping, and of the dagon and the child Elfwyth of the Erle Merle, and of the Boy and the borebel pit, and the Lady Gringold and her norange tree. And the damsel Ferly listened closely, her mouth opened in her listening, her hands clasped upon her knees. She gave a slow, deep sigh when he had done.

"Oh, it is a marvellous quest, falling into borebel

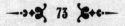

pits and being flown away by Lady-birds, all for the love of a weeping Damsen." Her hand crept gently upon Caerles' arm and her eyes were suddenly still and shy. "I will tell you a secret," she said. "There is a shepherd boy across the meadow who left a flower on a stone for me. . . ."

The Cnite smiled. "That is a marvellous thing, too," he said, and she smiled back.

"Yes." She jumped up then, and wrapped a long, patched cloak about her. "And now, I will give you your protection, since you are a true Cnite. I found it one day beneath the walls of the Dolorous House. Wait."

She opened the door and vanished suddenly into the singing, weeping winds. The Cnite Caerles rose and watched for her out of the open door. Things moved and howled beyond his eyesight, and great, invisible trees shivered and chattered like ghosts. Far away, above a black hill, tiny specks of strange-colored light flickered like the rich wings of butterflies.

Ferly returned finally, breathless, her hair

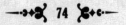

knotted and wet, her hands overflowing with an old sack. She knelt on the stone floor and opened the sack. A great cloak tumbled out, made of leaves of all colors, all shapes, sewn together with a thread of vine-stem. She held it out to him.

"It will protect you from all danger. And it will make you invisible."

Caerles took it slowly. "That is not possible."

"It is. Everything is possible. You will go in and out of the Dolorous House and not one evil eye will see you. Put it on!"

Caerles swung it about his shoulders. It settled, rustling softly, brushing the floor. He put the cloak over his head and looked at her. Ferly giggled suddenly behind her hands.

"Oh, it is marvellous. But that silvery shirt—you must take it off, because it will not disappear and it looks funny."

"But I will have no protection against blows from knife or sword," Caerles protested.

"You will not need it, because no one with a knife or sword will see you. Take it off."

Caerles pulled off his shirt of mail reluctantly, and stood unprotected in his dark doublet with three moons floating on it. He put the cloak of leaves back on and the damsel Ferly clasped her hands.

"Oh, yes! It is truly magic. Everything is magic on a quest for love. You will find your Throme. My bones feel it. And then you will go home and marry your Damsen because of my cloak of many leaves. Now you must go."

"But it is raining," Caerles said.

Ferly danced to the door and opened it to the starless night. Her voice hushed. "Adventure comes on nights like this, when the whole world is whispering magic. A true Cnite would not complain of a little rain."

"That is more than a little rain," Caerles argued, looking at it. Ferly turned to get his harp and his star-wand. She pushed them into his hands, and her eyes were dark and solemn.

"You must go now. My bones feel it. Think how wet your Damsen must be after all her weeping.

You must go for her wet sake. I saw the strange lights, tonight, and I know this is the night to slip secretly into a Doleman's House and steal his Throme."

Caerles sighed a dreary sigh. Then he said, "Thank you most deeply for your hearth and your help. If there is one thing I may do for you—"

"Oh, please," said Ferly, and her hands were folded in petition. "Please, there is a thing. May I—may I have your beautiful silver shirt? May I leave it for a shepherd boy, on a stone?"

Caerles smiled. "Oh yes," he said reluctantly.

The dagon mourned as it sped over the muddy road, turned through its twistings, while the trees arched across it, raging with the wind of their passing. At the third turning dark walls of stone rose on a hill against the smokey clouds, and strange wheels of color swirled above it. The road ran through the mouth of its gate.

The dagon lit a great door with the glow of its mouth. Caerles went to it softly and opened it. It cried at the opening like a wailing beast. A great

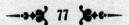

hall stood silent behind it, black but for a half-eaten log on a hearth.

A candle winked suddenly on Caerles' face. An old, hunched man with hollow eyes stared at him.

"Who are you?" His voice quivered like a loose harpstring. "What are you beneath that strange cloak?"

Caerles was still a moment. Then he pushed the hood back from his face and rubbed his eyes. "What house is this?"

"It is the House of the Lady Welman. Do you want shelter? Why did you not knock? You frightened my old heart."

"I am the Cnite Caerles in quest of the Throme of the Erril of Sherill. I was told this is the Dolorous House of the dead Doleman."

The old man shook his head. "I have heard tales of that House. It was said to stand here once. Some say they can still see it, and its strange lights, on nights like this, but I have never seen it. . . . Are you hungry? Come with me, and I will give you supper and a warm fire." He turned,

and led Caerles through the still hall. "Now, the Throme I have heard of, too. I think you will find it at the Western Wellsprings, beneath the setting sun. They say that is where Sherill is."

"They said also," Caerles said, "that it is in the Mirk-Well of Morg, at the Floral Wold, and in the Dolorous House of the dead Doleman."

The old man shook his head once. "No."

"No?"

"No. It is at the Western Wellsprings. That is where the Erril wrote it."

Caerles sighed.

SIX

And so the leaf-cloaked Cnite, the star-wand at his side and the harp at his back, rode the dagon with the morning winds to find the Throme at the Western Wellsprings. The storm had wept its fill and gone. Trees glittered with jewels of rain and clear puddles mirrored the moving sun. The Cnite rode slowly through the wet world, and tiny birds swooped in the air above his head and splashed in pools on the meadow-grasses. He made, in the morning world, a song for his Damsen and plucked it from the gold harp. The dagon howled with his singing, and tiny animals scurried, startled under hidden leaves. A

river wound out of nowhere and danced beside him, following. It widened as it moved, and its singing voice deepened as it tumbled over the heads of mossy rocks and shimmered into spinning pools. And suddenly it swept across his path, and the Cnite halted at its bank.

"Oh, Dracoberus," he murmured to the dagon, whose flaming tongue was lapping water, "I do not like swimming wet rivers." And he looked up and down the bank for a shallow place to cross, but the river was wide and deep and slow. Across the river a green wood grew of round, plump trees, tall trees like closed fans, and great old trees with strong, broad limbs swooping low over the green water, and high into the clear sky. Flowers gathered at their roots, red and bright sun yellow and purple as the dagon's eyes. And the wind, nestling among them, blew a sound across the water like sweet golden bells, and above the rippling water, high voices laughed in secret. The faint wind smelled of growing things. A thought opened like a flower in the Cnite's heart and he smiled slowly.

"Is it there?" he whispered. "Is it there the Erril's Throme of loveliness was written?" And he nudged the dagon forward, but it whimpered at the wide water's edge and danced away. "Oh, dagon," sighed the Cnite, "you have taken me this far. Can you not go a little farther, for my sake and my sweet Damsen's?"

The dagon barked at the river, and fire hissed and spattered in it. Far across the river, flowers jangled like soft bells, and the noon sun flickered in the green grass. The dagon barked again, but the water would not go away. Then a voice said beside them,

"I will take you across the river, Tree-Man, but there will be a price."

Caerles looked down. A man stood beside him with a pole, his shoulders broad, knotted like tree roots. His eyes were wide and cautious. Caerles said,

"I am a Cnite. Why do you call me a Tree-Man?"

"I have never seen so many living leaves without a tree," the young man said. "And I have never

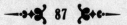

seen a Cnite without a sword or shield. And I
have never seen a Cnite ride a Thing like you are
riding. I will take you but I will not take That,
because it will burn my boat and that is all I own."

Caerles shook his head. "I will not go without
him. He does not belong to me, and I must keep
him safely and return him. What land is that,
beyond the river?"

"I do not know. People go across, and they do
not come back to tell me. A great King's court lies
beyond the trees, I have heard. Do you want to go
there? You must pay me. I am a poor man and I
have a wife and a son with no shoes."

"What do you want of me?" Caerles said. "I will
give you whatever you ask that belongs to me, for
I think beyond this river lies the ending of my
quest. But you must take the dagon across, too."

"I will take him if he does not bark. I do not
know if a Tree-Man has anything I will want."

"I am a Cnite," said Caerles, "and I can give you
a promise of jewels, though I have none with me."

"I can give you a promise of all the King's gold,"

the boatman said. "I do not want to offend a Tree-Man, but I have never seen a jewel and I do not believe in them. But there is one thing I believe in of yours."

"Ask it of me."

"Give me your mouse-colored boots for my son to wear."

Caerles bent slowly and took off his boots. He gave them to the man and sat on the dagon, bare-headed, barefoot, listening to the gentle wind while the man brought his boat to them. The river spun in whorls from his dipping oars as he rowed them across, and the water was green and still and bottomless beneath them. Birds chattered from the woods ahead and flicked like jewels from branch to branch. A singing rose, soft as sunlight beyond the wind, and the Cnite smiled, and the quiet dagon licked his face. The boat thumped softly in the shallows and the boatman leaped ashore and drew them in beneath the sighing trees.

"Fare well, Cnite," he said as Caerles stepped

on the land. "There are those who look for quest's endings, and others who are content with a pair of boots. I wish you your contentment." And he got back into the boat and shoved it away with a ripple of oar. Caerles moved forward among the flowers massed at his feet. Ahead of him the trees thinned, and a meadow grew, full of cows with silver bells. Beyond the meadow fields began, lined with new plowing, and in the distance, on a hill, sat the dark, closed stone walls of the castle of Magnus Thrall, King of Everywhere.

A sadness beat in Caerles' heart like the sudden ache of bruised bone. He sat down on a fallen tree, murmuring wordlessly of despair, and the dagon whimpered and licked his hands.

"Oh, dagon," he mourned finally, "now what shall I do? I have made a circle of my quest, and there seems no ending to it. I have failed my Damsen, for I am too weary to hope any longer. There is no Throme, and if it does exist, it is always just beyond my outstretched hand, just beyond my eyesight."

The leaves shook suddenly above him, as though they were laughing. He looked up and found a great tree full of children.

They looked down at him out of secret eyes, as they clung to smooth, strong branches. They were small, and simply dressed, and their clothes were colored like the deep hearts of flowers. The leaves rustled again, and a boy dropped to the Cnite's bare feet. His eyes were round as berries, and his hands were brown with earth.

"Why are you sad, Tree-Man?" he said, and his voice squeaked a little with fear. "Do you have a mother to tell you everything will be all right?"

"No," said Caerles, and the small boy vanished, suddenly as a bird. A girl called down to the Cnite, her hair short and curly, like a cap of sunlight.

"Climb our tree, Tree-Man, and you can see the whole world. Climb our tree, and you can see the sky, and you will not feel sad. I know. Come and sing with us."

"There is no song in me," said the Cnite.

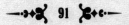

"Then we will sing to you," a black-eyed boy said, and their sweet voices rose and drifted down the wind.

A woman came running through the trees, wiping her hands on her apron as she followed the berry-eyed child. He stopped, pointing, in front of the Cnite.

"See—the Tree-Man and his Fire-Dog."

"He is sad," the Tree-Children called down and the bright-faced woman, her hair bound in a colored kerchief, smiled a little, and edged towards the Cnite.

"The dagon will not harm you," said Caerles, and she came to stand beside him by the log.

"There is no such thing as a tree-man," she said, and Caerles smiled.

"I am a Cnite," he said woefully, "on a quest for the Throme of the Erril of Sherill."

"There is no such thing," said the mother.

"I know, but if I do not find that Throme, I may not have the one thing I want: the sad-eyed Damsen of Magnus Thrall. That is why I am sad."

The sweet-eyed mother sat on the log beneath her child-tree. "But why are you barefoot, cloaked in leaves, with a harp at your back and a star at your side? I have seen Cnites and Cnites, but never a Cnite like you. They wear swords and shirts of metal and they ride horses, not dagons."

"I have been on a strange quest," said Caerles, and told her of it. The children were silent above him, their faces resting against the branches as they listened. The mother sighed when it was done.

"Oh, what a silly, wicked King to send you on such a quest, when he should have given his Damsen to you. But of course, there is one thing left to do."

"Is there?"

"Of course. You must write the Throme of the Erril of Sherill yourself."

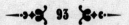

SEVEN

And so the Cnite Caerles wrote a
Throme, and it was a deep Throme and a dark,
haunting, lovely Throme, a wild, special sweet
Throme, made of the tales and dreams and hap-
penings of his quest. He sat beneath the child-tree
and wrote it, and the children played and sang
and called like birds from tree to tree. They sat on
the dagon's back and scratched its ears, and they
leaned against the Cnite and watched him write.
The mother brought them milk and bread beneath
the tree, and the Cnite ate and drank and kept
writing. The sun slipped finally behind the dark

house of Magnus Thrall, and the silver-belled cows went home across the cool meadow, and the weary children slipped away one by one to sleep. The Cnite put down his feather pen.

"It is a lie," he said.

"It is a Throme," said the mother, "and it is time for the King to give up his Damsen so that she can learn to laugh." She held the last waking child to her side, its face resting in her apron. Caerles smiled at the name she spoke.

"Yes." He stood up, rolling the Throme neatly, and the dagon sprang to its feet. "I will return now, to the King's house. One day, I will come back here with Damsen, and then I can give you fairly the thanks for your help today."

The mother smiled. "That will be fair thanks," she said.

"Goodbye, Tree-Man," said her child, yawning, and its plump small hand flashed in the twilight like a star.

The Cnite Caerles rode the silent-pawed dagon over the drawbridge of Magnus Thrall's house.

The dagon followed him up the dark, winding stairs, through the empty halls, past silent rooms to the last high room where firelight flashed red beneath the closed door and a gentle, broken voice sang behind it. The Cnite opened the door. The dark-robed shadow that was Magnus Thrall stopped its pacing before the fire. The needle and needlework dropped from Damsen's hands, and her face turned towards Caerles, pale and glistening, motionless with astonishment.

Then, suddenly, she began to laugh.

Her laughter was high and sweet and full, and the tears of it flashed like starlight in her eyes. She wiped them with her fingers and rose to touch the wordless Cnite.

"Oh, my Caerles," she said in laughter and tears. "Oh, my Caerles, you are barefoot. Why are you dressed in leaves like a tree-man? Where is your cloak? Did you really ride this dagon instead of your horse? Oh, my fair and proper Cnite, where are your mouse-colored boots?"

"Where," said the King, "is the Throme?"

"I have brought you the Throme," said Caerles.

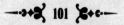

"And now you must keep your promise." He gave the King the rolled Throme, and looked into the wine-colored, laughing eyes of the King's Damsen.

"Yes," she said. "Yes. I never knew before how much I want a barefoot, leaf-cloaked Cnite. Oh, my Caerles, how did you find the Throme? It does not exist."

"I found it," said Caerles, and he put his hands on her face and looked deeply into her eyes.

Behind them the dark King whispered,

"The star-wand and the golden harp, the dark well, and the house of death, the jewel-eyed wiseman and the bottomless river and the flower wold at the world's end. . . . The Throme. It is the Throme!" His voice shouted suddenly like a trumpet. "Take Damsen for I no longer need her weeping, and my heart will no longer wail with longing for a thing which does not exist. I have the Throme! I will wake content to the sunlight and simple wind, open my doors to the chatter of

birds and churttels. I will be content with the green world, with the light that fades and the singing leaves that wither so quickly, for I have the Throme of such beauty that will never fade. I will make you my Chief Cnite—"

"I already am your Chief Cnite," said Caerles.

"I will give you fat lands and churttels to toil over them and a house more magnificent than mine for Damsen and your sons."

"And daughters," said Caerles.

"I will proclaim your name in every village and city as the Cnite who has done the impossible deed of finding the lost Throme of the Erril of Sherill."

Caerles sighed. "It is a lie," he said to the dark eyes of Damsen, and Magnus Thrall's voice stopped shouting and quivered.

"A lie?"

"I wrote the Throme. It is the Throme of the Cnite Caerles."

The night was silent within the dark King's

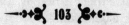

walls and without. The King stood still as the dark wood of an unlit torch. Damsen stopped smiling. Her mouth quivered.

"You wrote this Throme?" Magnus Thrall whispered.

"Yes."

"How did you write it?"

"Sitting under a child-tree, with paper and a feather pen."

"But I do not need a magnificent house," Damsen said wistfully. "I need this leaf-cloaked Cnite with a gentle voice."

Magnus Thrall stepped closer to them, his eyes flickering with firelight, his hands clasped tight around the Throme. "But where did you find the words for it? The names and dreams and colors for it?"

"Everywhere," said Caerles to Damsen's eyes.

"In my land you built this Throme?"

Caerles looked at him. "There was no place else to go. So I built a lie. And now, do what you will with me, because there is no place in the world to find that Throme you wanted."

The King of Everywhere took off his crown. He threw it against the stones and it bounced and spun and rolled into a corner. And then he took the rolled Throme of the Cnite Caerles and flung it into the fire, where little flames danced black across it.

"You lied to me!"

"I know," whispered Caerles.

"You failed your quest."

"I know."

"You tried to trick me with a false Throme, to slyly take my Damsen from me."

"But I love your Damsen," said Caerles helplessly, and Damsen, clinging to his leaf-cloaked arm, looked up at him with dry, midnight eyes. The dark King's shadow ran like withered ivy across the stone walls.

"There are Cnites and Cnites," he said. "There will be other Cnites to find the great Throme, other Cnites to love Damsen, to lead her into the green world. You are not my Cnite. You are a Tree-Man, with no shield but a silly harp, and no sword but a fading star. I must have the Throme

for the ease of my longing heart and I will wait for it in these dark rooms forever if I must, and my Damsen will wait here with me."

The Tree-Man Caerles sighed beneath his leaves. He sighed again, his leaves whispering, his eyes on the fading star of his Throme. He said softly, "Then I will go back and look again, forever if I must, and Damsen, if it pleases her, will wait here for me."

Damsen's mouth trembled. Then she straightened beside Caerles and her mouth went straight and taut as a new bow-string. "I will not," she said to him, and her eyes were dry as nights with a thousand stars. "I will not wither here in these stones." She turned to Magnus Thrall. "I do not care about your Throme. I want this moon-haired, barefoot Cnite, and I will have him, Throme or no Throme. I want to walk in the singing world. I want to laugh instead of weep. You can weep here alone. I will go with him." She turned back to Caerles and took his hands. "And you will write your Throme again for me. I have known a fair

and moon-colored Cnite with a horse and shield and I know a barefoot Tree-Man with a dagon and a star-wand, and I know which one sang a Throme to my heart to make it wake and laugh. I know, in all the worlds, there is no Throme more beautiful than the Throme of the Tree-Cnite Caerles."

Words gathered like tears in the Tree-Cnite's eyes. He shook his head, smiling through them. "No," he whispered. "There is one more beautiful Throme, and that is one I will write only for you, my Damsen."

"Bah," said Magnus Thrall. He looked at the dark, still walls around him. He kicked the fire to make it spark. Flames leaped upward, but still the shadows clung like cob-web to the silent corners. "You will regret it. He is no longer my Chief Cnite."

"He is mine," said Damsen.

"He brought back dishonor and failure from his quest, and he will have no place in my favor."

"There is no favor in you for anyone."

"From my stone walls to his stone walls you will go."

"No," said the Tree-Cnite quickly. "I know a place with quiet water and wind singing through trees, where I will build a house for you with flowers at your doorstep and cows with cow-bells in your field."

"I would like to hear a cow-bell," said Damsen.

"And together, if it pleases you, we will grow a great tree full of children."

His Damsen smiled. "I would like a child-tree."

"Cow-bells," said Magnus Thrall. "You will be sorry. You will leave him and come back and wait with me for a proper Cnite."

"I have a proper Cnite," said Damsen, and the Tree-Cnite lifted her onto the flower-eyed dagon. "And I will go Everywhere with him."

"Bah," said Magnus Thrall. The fiery breath of the dagon lit the dark, winding stones as Caerles led his Damsen into the sweet night-world of whispering grass and moonlit leaves. The King watched the fire-breath fade across the fields like

a dying star. In the fire, the ashes of the Tree-Cnite's Throme crumbled and drifted apart. The dark King stared at them and whispered in the stillness,

"Bah."

The Harrowing
of the
Dragon of Hoarsbreath

Once, on the top of a world, there existed the ring of an island named Hoarsbreath, made out of gold and snow. It was all mountain, a grim, briney, yellowing ice-world covered with winter twelve months out of thirteen. For one month, when the twin suns crossed each other at the world's cap, the snow melted from the peak of Hoarsbreath. The hardy trees shrugged the snow off their boughs, and sucked in light and mellow air, pulling themselves toward the suns. Snow and icicles melted off the roofs of the miners' village; the snow-tunnels they had dug from house

to tavern to storage barn to mineshaft sagged to the ground; the dead-white river flowing down from the mountain to the sea turned blue and began to move again. Then the miners gathered the gold they had dug by firelight out of the chill, harsh darkness of the deep mountain, and took it downriver, across the sea to the mainland, to trade for food and furs, tools and a liquid fire called wormspoor, because it was gold and bitter, like the leavings of dragons. After three swallows of it, in a busy city with a harbor frozen only part of the year, with people who wore rich furs, kept horses and sleds to ride in during winter, and who knew the patterns of the winter stars since they weren't buried alive by the snow, the miners swore they would never return to Hoarsbreath. But the gold waiting in the dark secret places of the mountain-island drew at them in their dreaming, lured them back.

For two hundred years after the naming of Hoarsbreath, winter followed winter, and the miners lived their rich, isolated, precarious lives

on the pinnacle of ice and granite, cursing the cold and loving it, for it kept lesser folk away. They mined, drank, spun tales, raised children who were sent to the mainland when they were half-grown, to receive their education, and find easier, respectable lives. But always a few children found their way back, born with a gnawing in their hearts for fire, ice, stone, and the solitary pursuit of gold in the dark.

Then, two miners' children came back from the great world and destroyed the island.

They had no intention of doing that. The younger of them was Peka Krao. After spending five years on the mainland, boring herself with schooling, she came back to Hoarsbreath to mine. At seventeen, she was good-natured and sturdy, with dark eyes, and dark, braided hair. She loved every part of Hoarsbreath, even its chill, damp shafts at midwinter and the bone-jarring work of hewing through darkness and stone to unbury its gold. Her instincts for gold were uncanny: she seemed to sense it through her

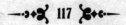

fingertips touching bare rock. The miners called her their good luck. She could make wormspoor, too, one of the few useful things she had learned on the mainland. It lost its bitterness, somehow, when she made it: it aged into a rich, smokey gold that made the miners forget their sore muscles, and inspired marvellous tales out of them that whittled away at the endless winter.

She met the Dragon-Harrower one evening at a cross-section of tunnel between her mother's house and the tavern. She knew all the things to fear in her world: a rumble in the mountain, a guttering torch in the mines, a crevice in the snow, a crack of ice underfoot. There was little else she couldn't handle with a soft word or her own right arm. So when he loomed out of the darkness unexpectedly into her taper-light, she wasn't afraid. But he made her stop instinctively, like an animal might stop, faced with something that puzzled its senses.

His hair was dead-white, with strands bright as wormspoor running through it; his eyes were the

 118

light, hard blue of dawn during suns-crossing. Rich colors flashed out of him everywhere in her light: from a gold knife-hilt and a brass pack buckle; from the red ties of his cloak that were weighted with ivory, and the blue and silver threads in his gloves. His heavy fur cloak was closed, but she felt that if he shifted, other colors would escape from it into the cold, dark air. At first she thought he must be ancient: the taper-fire showed her a face that was shadowed and scarred, remote with strange experience, but no more than a dozen years older than hers.

"Who are you?" she breathed. Nothing on Hoarsbreath glittered like that in midwinter; its colors were few and simple: snow, damp fur and leather, fire, gold.

"I can't find my father," he said. "Lule Yarrow."

She stared at him, amazed that his colors had their beginnings on Hoarsbreath. "He's dead." His eyes widened slightly, losing some of their hardness. "He fell in a crevice. They chipped him out of the ice at suns-crossing, and buried him six years ago."

He looked away from her a moment, down at the icy ridges of tramped snow. "Winter." He broke the word in two, like an icicle. Then he shifted his pack, sighing. "Do they still have wormspoor on this ice-tooth?"

"Of course. Who are you?"

"Ryd Yarrow. Who are you?"

"Peka Krao."

"Peka. I remember. You were squalling in somebody's arms when I left."

"You look a hundred years older than that," she commented, still puzzling, holding him in her light, though she was beginning to feel the cold. "Seventeen years you've been gone. How could you stand it, being away from Hoarsbreath so long? I couldn't stand five years of it. There are so many people whose names you don't know, trying to tell you about things that don't matter, and the flat earth and the blank sky are everywhere. Did you come back to mine?"

He glanced up at the grey-white ceiling of the snow-tunnel, barely an inch above his head. "The

sky is full of stars, and the gold wake of dragon-flights," he said softly. "I am a Dragon-Harrower. I am trained and hired to trouble dragons out of their lairs. That's why I came back here."

"Here. There are no dragons on Hoarsbreath."

His smile touched his eyes like a reflection of fire across ice. "Hoarsbreath is a dragon's heart."

She shifted, her own heart suddenly chilled. She said tolerantly, "That sounds like a marvellous tale to me."

"It's no tale. I know. I followed this dragon through centuries, through ancient writings, through legends, through rumors of terror and deaths. It is here, sleeping, coiled around the treasures of Hoarsbreath. If you on Hoarsbreath rouse it, you are dead. If I rouse it, I will end your endless winter."

"I like winter." Her protest sounded very small, muted within the thick snow-walls, but he heard it. He lifted his hand, held it lightly against the low ceiling above his head.

"You might like the sky beyond this. At night it

123

is a mine of lights and hidden knowledge."

She shook her head. "I like close places, full of fire and darkness. And faces I know. And tales spun out or wormspoor. If you come with me to the tavern, they'll tell you where your father is buried, and give you lodgings, and then you can leave."

"I'll come to the tavern. With a tale."

Her taper was nearly burned down, and she was beginning to shiver. "A dragon." She turned away from him. "No one will believe you anyway."

"You do."

She listened to him silently, warming herself with wormspoor, as he spoke to the circle of rough, fire-washed faces in the tavern. Even in the light, he bore little resemblance to his father, except for his broad cheekbones and the threads of gold in his hair. Under his bulky cloak, he was dressed as plainly as any miner, but stray bits of color still glinted from him, suggesting wealth and distant places.

"A dragon," he told them, "is creating your winter. Have you ever asked yourselves why winter

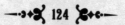

124

on this island is nearly twice as long as winter on the mainland twenty miles away? You live in dragon's breath, in the icy mist of its bowels, hoar-frost cold, that grips your land in winter the way another dragon's breath might burn it to flinders. One month out of the year, in the warmth of suns-crossing, it looses it's ring-grip on your island, slides into the sea, and goes to mate. Its ice-kingdom begins to melt. It returns, loops its length around its mountain of ice and gold. Its breath freezes the air once more, locks the river into its bed, you into your houses, the gold into its mountain, and you curse the cold and drink until the next dragon-mating." He paused. There was not a sound around him. "I've been to strange places in this world, places even colder than this, where the suns never cross, and I have seen such monsters. They are ancient as rock, white as old ice, and their skin is like iron. They breed winter and they cannot be killed. But they can be driven away, into far corners of the world where they are dangerous to no one. I'm trained for this. I can rid you of your winter. Harrowing is dangerous work,

and usually I am highly paid. But I've been looking for this ice-dragon for many years, through its spoor of legend and destruction. I tracked it here, one of the oldest of its kind, to the place where I was born. All I ask from you is a guide."

He stopped, waiting. Peka, her hands frozen around her glass, heard someone swallow. A voice rose and faded from the tavern-kitchen; sap hissed in the fire. A couple of the miners were smiling; the others looked satisfied and vaguely expectant, wanting the tale to continue. When it didn't, Kor Flynt, who had mined Hoarsbreath for fifty years, spat wormspoor into the fire. The flame turned a baleful gold, and then subsided. "Suns-crossing," he said politely, reminding a scholar of a scrap of knowledge children acquired with their first set of teeth, "causes the seasons."

"Not here," Ryd said. "Not on Hoarsbreath. I've seen. I know."

Peka's mother Ambris leaned forward. "Why," she asked curiously, "would a miner's son become a dragon-harrower?" She had a pleasant, craggy

face; her dark hair and her slow, musing voice were like Peka's. Peka saw the Dragon-Harrower ride between two answers in his mind. Meeting Ambris' eyes, he made a choice, and his own eyes strayed to the fire.

"I left Hoarsbreath when I was twelve. When I was fifteen, I saw a dragon in the mountains east of the city. Until then, I had intended to come back and mine. I began to learn about dragons. The first one I saw burned red and gold under the suns' fire; it swallowed small hills with its shadow. I wanted to call it, like a hawk. I wanted to fly with it. I kept studying, meeting other people who studied them, seeing other dragons. I saw a night-black dragon in the northern deserts; its scales were dusted with silver, and the flame that came out of it was silver. I saw people die in that flame, and I watched the harrowing of that dragon. It lives now on the underside of the world, in shadow. We keep watch on all known dragons. In the green mid-world belt, rich with rivers and mines, forests and farmland, I saw a whole mining

town burned to the ground by a dragon so bright I thought at first it was sun-fire arching down to the ground. Someone I loved had the task of tracking that one to its cave, deep beneath the mineshafts. I watched her die, there. I nearly died. The dragon is sealed into the bottom of the mountain, by stone and by words. That is the dragon which harrowed me." He paused to sip wormspoor. His eyes lifted, not to Ambris, but to Peka. "Now do you understand what danger you live in? What if one year the dragon sleeps through its matingtime, with the soft heat of the suns making it sluggish from dreaming? You don't know it's there, wrapped around your world. It doesn't know you're there, stealing its gold. What if you sail your boats full of gold downriver and find the great white bulk of it sprawled like a wall across your passage? Or worse, you find its eye opening like a third, dead sun to see your hands full of its gold? It would slide its length around the mountain, coil upward and crush you all, then breathe over the whole of the island, and turn it deadwhite as its heart, and it would never sleep again."

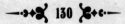

There was another silence. Peka felt something play along her spine like the thin, quavering, arthritic fingers of wind. "It's getting better," she said, "your tale." She took a deep swallow of wormspoor and added, "I love sitting in a warm, friendly place listening to tales I don't have to believe."

Kor Flynt shrugged. "It rings true, lass."

"It is true," Ryd said.

"Maybe so," she said. "And it may be better if you just let the dragon sleep."

"And if it wakes unexpectedly? The winter killed my father. The dragon at the heart of winter could destroy you all."

"There are other dangers. Rock falls, sudden floods, freezing winds. A dragon is simply one more danger to live with."

He studied her. "I saw a dragon once with wings as softly blue as a spring sky. Have you ever felt spring on Hoarsbreath? It could come."

She drank again. "You love them," she said. "Your voice loves them and hates them, Dragon-Harrower."

—◆◆ 131 ◆◆—

"I hate them," he said flatly. "Will you guide me down the mountain?"

"No. I have work to do."

He shifted, and the colors rippled from him again, red, gold, silver, spring-blue. She finished the wormspoor, felt it burn in her like liquid gold. "It's only a tale. All your dragons are just colors in our heads. Let the dragon sleep. If you wake it, you'll destroy the night."

"No," he said. "You will see the night. That's what you're afraid of."

Kor Flynt shrugged. "There probably is no dragon, anyway."

"Spring, though," Ambris said; her face had softened. "Sometimes I can smell it from the mainland, and I always wonder . . . Still, after a hard day's work, sitting beside a roaring fire sipping dragon-spit, you can believe anything. Especially this." She looked into her glass at the glowering liquid. "Is this some of yours, Peka? What did you put into it?"

"Gold." The expression in Ryd's eyes made her swallow sudden tears of frustration. She refilled

her glass. "Fire, stone, dark, wood-smoke, night air smelling like cold tree-bark. You don't care, Ryd Yarrow."

"I do care," he said imperturbably. "It's the best wormspoor I've ever tasted."

"And I put a dragon's heart into it." She saw him start slightly; ice and hoar-frost shimmered from him. "If that's what Hoarsbreath is." A dragon beat into her mind, its wings of rime, its breath smoldering with ice, the guardian of winter. She drew breath, feeling the vast bulk of it looped around them all, dreaming its private dreams. Her bones seemed suddenly fragile as kindling, and the gold wormspoor in her hands a guilty secret. "I don't believe it," she said, lifting her glass. "It's a tale."

"Oh, go with him, lass," her mother said tolerantly. "There may be no dragon, but we can't have him swallowed up in the ice like his father. Besides, it may be a chance for spring."

"Spring is for flatlanders. There are things that shouldn't be wakened. I know."

"How?" Ryd asked.

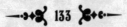

She groped, wishing for the first time for a flatlander's skill with words. She said finally, "I feel it," and he smiled. She sat back in her chair, irritated and vaguely frightened. "Oh, all right, Ryd Yarrow, since you'll go with or without me. I'll lead you down to the shores in the morning. Maybe by then you'll listen to me."

"You can't see beyond your snow-world," he said implacably. It is morning."

They followed one of the deepest mine-shafts, and clambered out of it to stand in the snow half-way down the mountain. The sky was lead grey; across the mists ringing the island's shores, they could see the ocean, a swirl of white, motionless ice. The mainland harbor was locked. Peka wondered if the ships were stuck like birds in the ice. The world looked empty and somber.

"At least in the dark mountain there is fire and gold. Here, there isn't even a sun." She took out a skin of wormspoor, sipped it to warm her bones. She held it out to Ryd, but he shook his head.

"I need all my wits. So do you, or we'll both end up preserved in ice at the bottom of a crevice."

"I know. I'll keep you safe." She corked the skin and added, "In case you were wondering."

But he looked at her, startled out of his remoteness. "I wasn't. Do you feel that strongly?"

"Yes."

"So did I, when I was your age. Now I feel very little." He moved again. She stared after him, wondering how he kept her smoldering and on edge. She said abruptly, catching up with him,

"Ryd Yarrow."

"Yes."

"You have two names. Ryd Yarrow, and Dragon-Harrower. One is a plain name this mountain gave you. The other you got from the world, the name that gives you color. One name I can talk to, the other is the tale at the bottom of a bottle of wormspoor. Maybe you could understand me if you hadn't brought your past back to Hoarsbreath."

"I do understand you," he said absently. "You

135

want to sit in the dark all your life and drink wormspoor."

She drew breath and held it. "You talk but you don't listen," she said finally. "Just like all the other flatlanders." He didn't answer. They walked in silence awhile, following the empty bed of an old river. The world looked dead, but she could tell by the air, which was not even freezing spangles of breath on her hood-fur, that the winter was drawing to an end. "Suns-crossing must be only two months away," she commented surprisedly.

"Besides, I'm not a flatlander," he said abruptly, surprising her again. "I do care about the miners, about Hoarsbreath. It's because I care that I want to challenge that ice-dragon with all the skill I possess. Is it better to let you live surrounded by danger, in bitter cold, carving half-lives out of snow and stone, so that you can come fully alive for one month of the year?"

"You could have asked us."

"I did ask you."

She sighed. "Where will it live, if you drive it away from Hoarsbreath?"

He didn't answer for a few paces. In the still day, he loosed no colors, though Peka thought she saw shadows of them around his pack. His head was bowed; his eyes were burning back at a memory. "It will find some strange, remote places where there is no gold, only rock; it can ring itself around emptiness and dream of its past. I came across an ice-dragon unexpectedly once, in a land of ice. The bones of its wings seemed almost translucent. I could have sworn it cast a white shadow."

"Did you want to kill it?"

"No. I loved it."

"Then why do you—" But he turned at her suddenly, almost angrily, waking out of a dream.

"I came here because you've built your lives on top of a terrible danger, and I asked for a guide, not a gad-fly."

"You wanted me," she said flatly. "And you don't care about Hoarsbreath. All you want is that

dragon. Your voice is full of it. What's a gad-fly?"

"Go ask a cow. Or a horse. Or anything else that can't live on this forsaken, frostbitten lump of ice."

"Why should you care, anyway? You've got the whole great world to roam in. Why do you care about one dragon wrapped around the tiny island on the top of nowhere?"

"Because it's beautiful and deadly and wrapped around my heartland. And I don't know—I don't know at the end of things which of us will be left on Hoarsbreath." She stared at him. He met her eyes fully. "I'm very skilled. But that is one very powerful dragon."

She whirled, fanning snow. "I'm going back. Find your own way to your harrowing. I hope it swallows you."

His voice stopped her. "You'll always wonder. You'll sit in the dark, drinking wormspoor twelve months out of thirteen, wondering what happened to me. What an ice-dragon looks like, on a winter's day, in full flight."

She hovered between two steps. Then, furiously, she followed him.

They climbed deeper into mist, and then into darkness. They camped at night, ate dried meat and drank wormspoor beside a fire in the snow. The night-sky was sullen and starless as the day. They woke to grey mists and travelled on. The cold breathed up around them; walls of ice, yellow as old ivory, loomed over them. They smelled the chill, sweaty smell of the sea. The dead riverbed came to an end over an impassible cliff. They shifted ground, followed a frozen stream downward. The ice-walls broke up into great jewels of ice, blue, green, gold, massed about them like a giant's treasure hoard. Peka stopped to stare at them. Ryd said with soft, bitter satisfaction,

"Wormspoor."

She drew breath. "Wormspoor." Her voice sounded small, absorbed by cold. "Ice-jewels, fallen stars. Down here you could tell me anything and I might believe it. I feel very strange." She uncorked the wormspoor and took a healthy swig.

Ryd reached for it, but he only rinsed his mouth and spat. His face was pale; his eyes red-rimmed, tired.

"How far down do you think we are?"

"Close. There's no dragon. Just mist." She shuddered suddenly at the soundlessness. "The air is dead. Like stone. We should reach the ocean soon."

"We'll reach the dragon first."

They descended hillocks of frozen jewels. The stream they followed fanned into a wide, skeletal filigree of ice and rock. The mist poured around them, so painfully cold it burned their lungs. Peka pushed fur over her mouth, breathed through it. The mist or wormspoor she had drunk was forming shadows around her, flickerings of faces and enormous wings. Her heart felt heavy; her feet dragged like boulders when she lifted them. Ryd was coughing mist; he moved doggedly, as if into a hard wind. The stream fanned again, going very wide before it met the sea. They stumbled down into a bone-searing flow of mist. Ryd disappeared; Peka found him again, bumping into him, for he

had stopped. The threads of mist untangled above them, and she saw a strange black sun, hodded with a silvery web. As she blinked at it, puzzled, the web rolled up. The dark sun gazed back at her. She became aware then of her own heartbeat, of a rhythm in the mists, of a faint, echoing pulse all around her: the icy heartbeat of Hoarsbreath.

She drew a hiccup of a breath, stunned. There was a mountain-cave ahead of them, from which the mists breathed and eddied. Icicles dropped like bars between its grainy-white surfaces. Within it rose stones or teeth as milky white as quartz. A wall of white stretched beyond the mists, vast, earthworm round, solid as stone. She couldn't tell in the blur and welter of mist, where winter ended and the dragon began.

She made a sound. The vast, silvery eyelid drooped like a parchment unrolled, then lifted again. From the depths of the cave came a faint, rumbling, a vague, drowsy waking question: Who?

She heard Ryd's breath finally. "Look at the

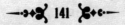

scar under its eye," he said softly. She saw a jagged track beneath the black sun. "I can name the Harrower who put that there three hundred years ago. And the broken eyetooth. It razed a marble fortress with its wings and jaws; I know the word that shattered that tooth, then. Look at its wing-scales. Rimed with silver. It's old. Old as the world." He turned finally, to look at her. His white hair, slick with mists, made him seem old as winter. "You can go back now. You won't be safe here."

"I won't be safe up there, either," she whispered. "Let's both go back. Listen to its heart."

"Its blood is gold. Only one Harrower ever saw that and lived."

"Please." She tugged at him, at his pack. Colors shivered into the air: sulphur, malachite, opal. The deep rumble came again; a shadow quickened in the dragon's eye. Ryd moved quickly, caught her hands. "Let it sleep. It belongs here on Hoarsbreath. Why can't you see that? Why can't you see? It's a thing made of gold, snow, darkness—" But he wasn't seeing her; his eyes,

142

remote and alien as the black sun, were full of memories and calculations. Behind him, a single curved claw lay like a crescent moon half-buried in the snow.

Peka stepped back from the Harrower, envisioning a bloody moon through his heart, and the dragon roused to fury, coiling upward around Hoarsbreath, crushing the life out of it. "Ryd Yarrow," she whispered. "Ryd Yarrow. Please." But he did not hear his name.

He began to speak, startling echoes against the solid ice around them. "Dragon of Hoarsbreath, whose wings are of hoarfrost, whose blood is gold—" The backbone of the hoar-dragon rippled slightly, shaking away snow. "I have followed your path of destruction from your beginnings in a land without time and without seasons. You have slept one night too long on this island. Hoarsbreath is not your dragon's dream; it belongs to the living, and I, trained and titled Dragon-Harrower, challenge you for its freedom." More snow shook away from the dragon, baring a rippling of scale, and the glistening of its nostrils. The

rhythm of its mist was changing. "I know you," Ryd continued, his voice growing husky, strained against the silence. "You were the white death of the fishing-island Klonos, of ten Harrowers in Ynyme, of the winter palace of the ancient lord of Zuirsh. I have harried nine ice-dragons—perhaps your children—out of the known world. I have been searching for you for many years, and I came back to the place where I was born to find you here. I stand before you armed with knowledge, experience, and the dark wisdom of necessity. Leave Hoarsbreath, go back to your birthplace forever, or I will harry you down to the frozen shadow of the world."

The dragon gazed at him motionlessly, an immeasurable ring of ice looped about him. The mist out of its mouth was for a moment suspended. Then its jaws crashed together, spitting splinters of ice. It shuddered, wrenched itself loose from the ice. Its white head reared high, higher, ice booming and cracking around it. Twin black suns stared down at Ryd from the grey mist of the sky. Before it roared, Peka moved.

She found herself on a ledge above Ryd's head, without remembering how she got there. Ryd vanished in a flood of mist. The mist turned fiery; Ryd loomed out of them like a red shadow, dispersing them. Seven crescents lifted out of the snow, slashed down at him, scarring the air. A strange voice shouted Ryd's name. He flung back his head and cried a word. Somehow the claw missed him, wedged deep into the ice.

Peka sat back. She was clutching the skin of wormspoor against her heart; she could feel her heartbeat shaking it. Her throat felt raw; the strange voice had been hers. She uncorked the skin, took a deep swallow, and another. Fire licked down her veins. A cloud of ice billowed at Ryd. He said something else, and suddenly he was ten feet away from it, watching a rock where he had stood freeze and snap into pieces.

Peka crouched closer to the wall of ice behind her. From her high point she could see the briny, frozen snarl of the sea. It flickered green, then an eerie orange. Bands of color pinioned the dragon briefly like a rainbow, arching across its wings. A

scale caught fire; a small bone the size of Ryd's forearm snapped. Then the cold wind of the dragon's breath froze and shattered the rainbow. A claw slapped at Ryd; he moved a fraction of a moment too slowly. The tip of a talon caught his pack. It burst open with an explosion of glittering colors. The dragon hooded its eyes; Peka hid hers under her hands. She heard Ryd cry out in pain. Then he was beside her instead of in several pieces, prying the wormspoor out of her hands.

He uncorked it, his hands shaking. One of them was seared silver.

"What are they?" she breathed. He poured wormspoor on his burned hand, then thrust it into the snow. The colors were beginning to die down.

"Flame," he panted. "Dragon-flame. I wasn't prepared to handle it."

"You carry it in your pack?"

"Caught in crystals, in fire-leaves. It will be more difficult than I anticipated."

Peka felt language she had never used before clamor in her throat. "It's all right," she said dourly. "I'll wait."

For a moment, as he looked at her, there was a memory of fear in his eyes. "You can walk across the ice to the mainland from here."

"You can walk to the mainland," she retorted. "This is my home. I have to live with or without that dragon. Right now, there's no living with it. You woke it out of its sleep. You burnt its wing. You broke its bone. You told it there are people on its island. You are going to destroy Hoars-breath."

"No. This will be my greatest harrowing." He left her suddenly, and appeared flaming like a torch on the dragon's skull, just between its eyes. His hair and his hands spattered silver. Word after word came out of him, smoldering, flashing, melting in the air. The dragon's voice thundered; its skin rippled and shook. Its claw ripped at ice, dug chasms out of it. The air clapped nearby, as if its invisible tail had lifted and slapped at the ground. Then it heaved its head, flung Ryd at the wall of mountain. Peka shut her eyes. But he fell lightly, caught up a crystal as he rose, and sent a shaft of piercing gold light at the upraised scales

147

of its underside, burrowing toward its heart.

Peka got unsteadily to her feet, her throat closing with a sudden whimper. But the dragon's tail, flickering out of the mist behind Ryd, slapped him into a snowdrift twenty feet away. It gave a cold, terrible hiss; mist bubbled over everything, so that for a few minutes Peka could see nothing beyond the lip of the ledge. She drank to stop her shivering. Finally a green fire blazed within the white swirl. She sat down again slowly, waited.

Night rolled in from the sea. But Ryd's fires shot in raw, dazzling streaks across the darkness, illuminating the hoary, scarred bulk of dragon in front of him. Once, he shouted endless poetry at the dragon, lulling it until its mist-breath was faint and slow from its maw. It nearly put Peka to sleep, but Ryd's imperceptible steps closer and closer to the dragon kept her watching. The tale was evidently an old one to the dragon; it didn't wait for an ending. Its head lunged and snapped unexpectedly, but a moment too soon. Ryd leaped for shelter in the dark, while the dragon's teeth ground painfully on nothingness. Later, Ryd

sang to it, a whining, eerie song that showered icicles around Peka's head. One of the dragon's teeth cracked, and it made an odd, high-pitched noise. A vast webbed wing shifted free to fly, unfolding endlessly over the sea. But the dragon stayed, sending mist at Ryd to set him coughing. A foul, ashy-grey miasma followed it, blurring over them. Peka hid her face in her arms. Sounds like the heaving of boulders and the spattering of fire came from beneath her. She heard the dragon's dry roar, like stones dragged against one another. There was a smack, a musical shower of breaking icicles, and a sharp, anguished curse. Ryd appeared out of the turmoil of light and air, sprawled on the ledge beside Peka.

His face was cut, with ice she supposed, and there was blood in his white hair. He looked at her with vague amazement.

"You're still here."

"Where else would I be? Are you winning or losing?"

He scooped up snow, held it against his face. "I feel as if I've been fighting for a thousand years . . .

Sometimes, I think I tangle in its memories, as it thinks of other harrowers, old dragon-battles, distant places. It doesn't remember what I am, only that I will not let it sleep . . . Did you see its wingspan? I fought a red dragon once with such a span. Its wings turned to flame in the sunlight. You'll see this one in flight by dawn."

She stared at him numbly, huddled against herself. "Are you so sure?"

"It's old and slow. And it can't bear the gold fire." He paused, then dropped the snow in his hand with a sigh, and leaned his face against the ice-wall. "I'm tired, too. I have one empty crystal, to capture the essence of its mist, its heart's breath. After that's done, the battle will be short." He lifted his head at her silence, as if he could hear her thoughts. "What?"

"You'll go on to other dragons. But all I've ever had is this one."

"You never know—"

"It doesn't matter that I never knew it. I know now. It was coiled all around us in the winter,

while we lived in warm darkness and firelight. It kept out the world. Is that such a terrible thing? Is there so much wisdom in the flatlands that we can't live without?"

He was silent again, frowning a little, either in pain or faint confusion. "It's a dangerous thing, a destroyer."

"So is winter. So is the mountain, sometimes. But they're also beautiful. You are full of so much knowledge and experience that you forgot how to see simple things. Ryd Yarrow, miner's son. You must have loved Hoarsbreath once."

"I was a child, then."

She sighed. "I'm sorry I brought you down here. I wish I were up there with the miners, in the last peaceful night."

"There will be peace again," he said, but she shook her head wearily.

"I don't feel it." She expected him to smile, but his frown deepened. He touched her face suddenly with his burned hand.

"Sometimes I almost hear what you're trying to

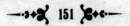

tell me. And then it fades against all my knowledge and experience. I'm glad you stayed. If I die, I'll leave you facing one maddened dragon. But still, I'm glad."

A black moon rose high over his shoulder and she jumped. Ryd rolled off the ledge, into the mists. Peka hid her face from the peering black glare. Blue light smoldered through the mist, the moon rolled suddenly out of the sky and she could breathe again.

Streaks of dispersing gold lit the dawn-sky like the sunrises she saw one month out of the year. Peka, in a cold daze on the ledge, saw Ryd for the first time in an hour. He was facing the dragon, his silver hand outstretched. In his palm lay a crystal so cold and deathly white that Peka, blinking at it, felt its icy stare into her heart.

She shuddered. Her bones turned to ice; mist seemed to flow through her veins. She breathed bitter, frozen air as heavy as water. She reached for the wormspoor; her arm moved sluggishly, and her fingers unfolded with brittle movements.

The dragon was breathing in short, harsh spurts. The silvery hoods were over its eyes. Its unfolded wing lay across the ice like a limp sail. Its jaws were open, hissing faintly, but its head was reared back, away from Ryd's hand. Its heartbeat, in the silence, was slow, slow.

Peka dragged herself up, icicle by icicle. In the clear wintry dawn, she saw the beginning and the end of the enormous ring around Hoarsbreath. The dragon's tail lifted wearily behind Ryd, then fell again, barely making a sound. Ryd stood still; his eyes, relentless, spring-blue, were his only color. As Peka watched, swaying on the edge, the world fragmented into simple things: the edges of silver on the dragon's scales, Ryd's silver fingers, his old-man's hair, the pure white of the dragon's hide. They faced one another, two powerful creatures born out of the same winter, harrowing one another. The dragon rippled along its bulk; its head reared farther back, giving Peka a dizzying glimpse of its open jaws. She saw the cracked tooth, crumbled like a jewel she might have bat-

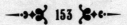

tered inadvertently with her pick, and winced.
Seeing her, it hissed, a tired, angry sigh.

She stared down at it; her eyes seemed numb,
incapable of sorrow. The wing on the ice was
beginning to stir. Ryd's head lifted. He looked
bone-pale, his face expressionless with exhaus-
tion. But the faint, icy smile of triumph in his eyes
struck her as deeply as the stare from the death-
eye in his palm.

She drew in mist like the dragon, knowing that
Ryd was not harrowing an old, tired ice-dragon,
but one out of his memories who never seemed to
yield. "You bone-brained dragon," she shouted,
"how can you give up Hoarsbreath so easily? And
to a Dragon-Harrower whose winter is colder
and more terrible than yours." Her heart seemed
trapped in the weary, sluggish pace of its heart.
She knelt down, wondering if it could understand
her words, or only feel them. "Think of Hoarsbreath," she pleaded, and searched for words to
warm them both. "Fire. Gold. Night. Warm
dreams, winter tales, silence—" Mist billowed at

her and she coughed until tears froze on her cheeks. She heard Ryd call her name on a curious, inflexible note that panicked her. She uncorked the wormspoor with trembling fingers, took a great gulp, and coughed again as the blood shocked through her. "Don't you have any fire at all in you? Any winter flame?" Then a vision of gold shook her; the gold within the dragon's heart, the warm gold of wormspoor, the bitter gold of dragon's blood. Ryd said her name again, his voice clear as breaking ice. She shut her eyes against him, her hands rising through a chill, dark dream. As he called the third time, she dropped the wormspoor down the dragon's throat.

The hoods over its eyes rose; they grew wide, white-rimmed. She heard a convulsive swallow. Its head snapped down; it made a sound between a bellow and a whimper. Then its jaws opened again and it raked the air with gold flame.

Ryd, his hair and eyebrows scored suddenly with gold, dove into the snow. The dragon hissed at him again. The stream beyond him turned fiery,

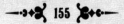

ran toward the sea. The great tail pounded furiously; dark cracks tore through the ice. The frozen cliffs began to sweat under the fire; pillars of ice sagged down, broke against the ground. The ledge Peka stood on crumbled at a wave of gold. She fell with it in a small avalanche of ice-rubble. The enormous white ring of dragon began to move, blurring endlessly past her eyes as the dragon gathered itself. A wing arched up toward the sky, then another. The dragon hissed at the mountain, then roared desperately, but only flame came out of its bowels, where once it had secreted winter. The chasms and walls of ice began breaking apart. Peka, struggling out of the snow, felt a lurch under her feet. A wind sucked at her hair, pulled at her heavy coat. Then it drove down at her, thundering, and she sat in the snow. The dragon, aloft, its wingspan the span of half the island, breathed fire at the ocean, and its husk of ice began to melt.

Ryd pulled her out of the snow. The ground was breaking up under their feet. He said nothing; she thought he was scowling, though he looked

strange with singed eyebrows. He pushed at her, flung her toward the sea. Fire sputtered around them. Ice slid under her; she slipped and clutched at the jagged rim of it. Brine splashed in her face. The ice whirled, as chunks of the mountain fell into the sea around them. The dragon was circling the mountain, melting huge peaks and cliffs. They struck the water hard, heaving the ice-floes farther from the island. The mountain itself began to break up, as ice tore away from it, leaving only a bare peak riddled with mine-shafts.

Peka began to cry. "Look what I've done. Look at it." Ryd only grunted. She thought she could see figures high on the top of the peak, staring down at the vanishing island. The ocean, churning, spun the ice-floe toward the mainland. The river was flowing again, a blue-white streak spiralling down from the peak. The dragon was over the mainland now, billowing fire at the harbor, and ships without crews or cargo were floating free.

"Wormspoor," Ryd muttered. A wave ten feet high caught up with them, spilled, and shoved

them into the middle of the channel. Peka saw the first of the boats taking the swift, swollen current down from the top of the island. Ryd spat out seawater, and took a firmer grip of the ice. "I lost every crystal, every dragon's fire I possessed. They're at the bottom of the sea. Thanks to you. Do you realize how much work, how many years—"

"Look at the sky." It spun above her, a pale, impossible mass of nothing. "How can I live under that? Where will I ever find dark, quiet places full of gold?"

"I held that dragon. It was just about to leave quietly, without taking half of Hoarsbreath with it."

"How will we live on the island again? All its secrets are gone."

"For fourteen years I studied dragons, their lore, their flights, their fires, the patterns of their lives and their destructions. I had all the knowledge I thought possible for me to acquire. No one—"

"Look at all that dreary flatland—"

"No one," he said, his voice rising, "ever told me

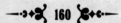

you could harrow a dragon by pouring worms-poor down its throat!"

"Well, no one told me, either!" She slumped beside him, too despondent for anger. She watched more boats carrying miners, young children, her mother, down to the mainland. Then the dragon caught her eye, pale against the winter sky, somehow fragile, beautifully crafted, flying into the wake of its own flame.

It touched her mourning heart with the fire she had given it. Beside her, she felt Ryd grow quiet. His face, tired and battered, held a young, forgotten wonder, as he watched the dragon blaze across the world's cap like a star, searching for its winter. He drew a soft, incredulous breath.

"What did you put into that wormspoor?"

"Everything."

He looked at her, then turned his face toward Hoarsbreath. The sight made him wince. "I don't think we left even my father's bones at peace," he said hollowly, looking for a moment less a Dragon-Harrower than a harrowed miner's son.

"I know," she whispered.

"No, you don't," he sighed. "You feel. The dragon's heart. My heart. It's not a lack of knowledge or experiences that destroyed Hoarsbreath, but something else I lost sight of: you told me that. The dark necessity of wisdom."

She gazed at him, suddenly uneasy, for he was seeing her. "I'm not wise. Just lucky—or unlucky."

"Wisdom is a flatlander's word for your kind of feeling. You put your heart into everything—wormspoor, dragons, gold—and they become a kind of magic."

"I do not. I don't understand what you're talking about, Ryd Yarrow. I'm a miner; I'm going to find another mine—"

"You have a gold-mine in your heart. There are other things you can do with yourself. Not harrow dragons, but become a Watcher. You love the same things they love."

"Yes. Peace and quiet and private places—"

"I could show you dragons in their beautiful, private places all over the world. You could speak their language."

"I can't even speak my own. And I hate the flatland." She gripped the ice, watching it come.

"The world is only another tiny island, ringed with a great dragon of stars and night."

She shook her head, not daring to meet his eyes. "No. I'm not listening to you anymore. Look what happened the last time I listened to your tales."

"It's always yourself you are listening to," he said. The grey ocean swirled the ice under them, casting her back to the bewildering shores of the world. She was still trying to argue when the ice moored itself against the scorched pilings of the harbor.

About the Author

Patricia A. McKillip was born on a leap year in Salem, Oregon, and grew up both in America and overseas. She is the author of seven books for young adults: *The Throme of the Erril of Sherill; The Night Gift; The House on Parchment Street; The Forgotten Beasts of Eld* (for which she won the World Fantasy Award); *The Riddlemaster of Hed; Heir of Sea and Fire;* and *Harpist in the Wind* (nominated for the Hugo Award). Her most recent work is an adult mainstream title with fantastic overtones titled *Stepping From the Shadows.* Ms. McKillip lives in San Francisco, California.

About the Artist

Judith Mitchell was born on Manhattan's Upper West Side to a family of music professors and still works best to musical accompaniment. Illustration was a perpetual pastime from earliest childhood to college. She graduated from Chatham College with a BFA and her studies at the School of Visual Arts were particularly encouraging while she talked herself into working as a freelance illustrator. She works very full time with the help of her husband Jack Murray, and three middle-aged cats who sometimes add pawprints to works they consider incomplete.

Do you dream of dragons? Would you like to work magic?
Or travel between worlds in the blink of an eye?
Would you like to see faeries dance,
or the place where baby unicorns are born?

COME ON A

MAGICQUEST ™

In these magical adventures
for kids from eight to eighty from
Tempo/MagicQuest Books:

#1. THE THROME OF THE ERRIL OF SHERILL,
Patricia A. McKillip

*The Throme of the Erril of Sherill — a book of songs
more beautiful than the stars themselves — does not
exist. Everyone knows that. But if Caerles is to win
his lady love, the sad-eyed daughter of the
King of Everywhere, he must find the Throme,
and so he sets out on an impossible quest.
Here's magical adventure from one of the most
popular fantasy writers since J.R.R. Tolkien — and
there are beautiful illustrations and a
special bonus dragon story too!*

___80839-5 — $2.25

#2. THE PERILOUS GARD, Elizabeth Marie Pope

*Kate is lonely. Banished by the Queen of England
to the Perilous Gard, a remote castle in Scotland,
she has no one to talk to all day but the moody,
mysterious young man whose brother owns the Gard.
But when she follows him into the world of faeries
she must do battle with the queen of Faery herself
to get him out again! This romantic fantasy won
a Newbery Honor.*

___65956-X — $2.25

#3. **THE SEVENTH SWAN**, Nicholas Stuart Gray

*There is a fairy tale about seven brothers
who are turned into swans by their evil stepmother.
Their sister turns them back into men
by knitting coats of nettles — but she doesn't
finish the sleeve of one coat in time
and at the end of the story the poor youngest brother
is left with a swan's wing in place of one arm.
Did you ever wonder what happened to him after that?
This book will tell you!*

—75955-6—$2.25

#4. **THE ASH STAFF**, Paul R. Fisher

*Mole is the oldest of six kids who were raised in a cave
by an old sorcerer in the magical land of Mon Ceth.
When the sorcerer dies, Mole must take up the ash staff
and become the group's leader.
This is the first of four books telling of their adventures
and their battle against the evil sorcerer
who has taken over their kingdom.
Paul R. Fisher was still a teenager himself
when he began the Ash Staff series.
If you are looking for something to read after Tolkien
or Lloyd Alexander — try Mole and his friends.*

—03115-3—$2.25

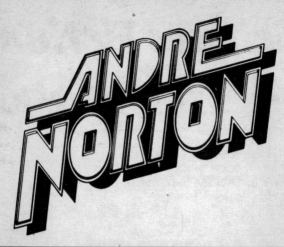

ANDRE NORTON